Based on the teleplay "Mojo Rising" by Jeremy Shipp

Cover drawn by Patrick Spaziante, color by Nickelodeon Studio

Interior illustrated by Nino Navarra

Random House 🏠 New York

© 2013 Viacom International Inc. and Viacom Overseas Holdings C.V. All rights reserved.
Published in the United States by Random House Children's Books, a division of Random House, Inc.,
1745 Broadway, New York, NY 10019, and in Canada by Random House of Canada Limited, Toronto.
Random House and the colophon are registered trademarks of Random House, Inc. Nickelodeon,
Teenage Mutant Ninja Turtles, and all related titles logos, and characters are trademarks
of Viacom International Inc. and Viacom Overseas Holdings C.V.
Based on characters created by Peter Laird and Kevin Eastman.
ISBN: 978-0-307-98229-2
randomhouse.com/kids
Manufactured in China
10 9 8 7 6 5
Glow Art and Production: Red Bird Publishing Ltd., UK.

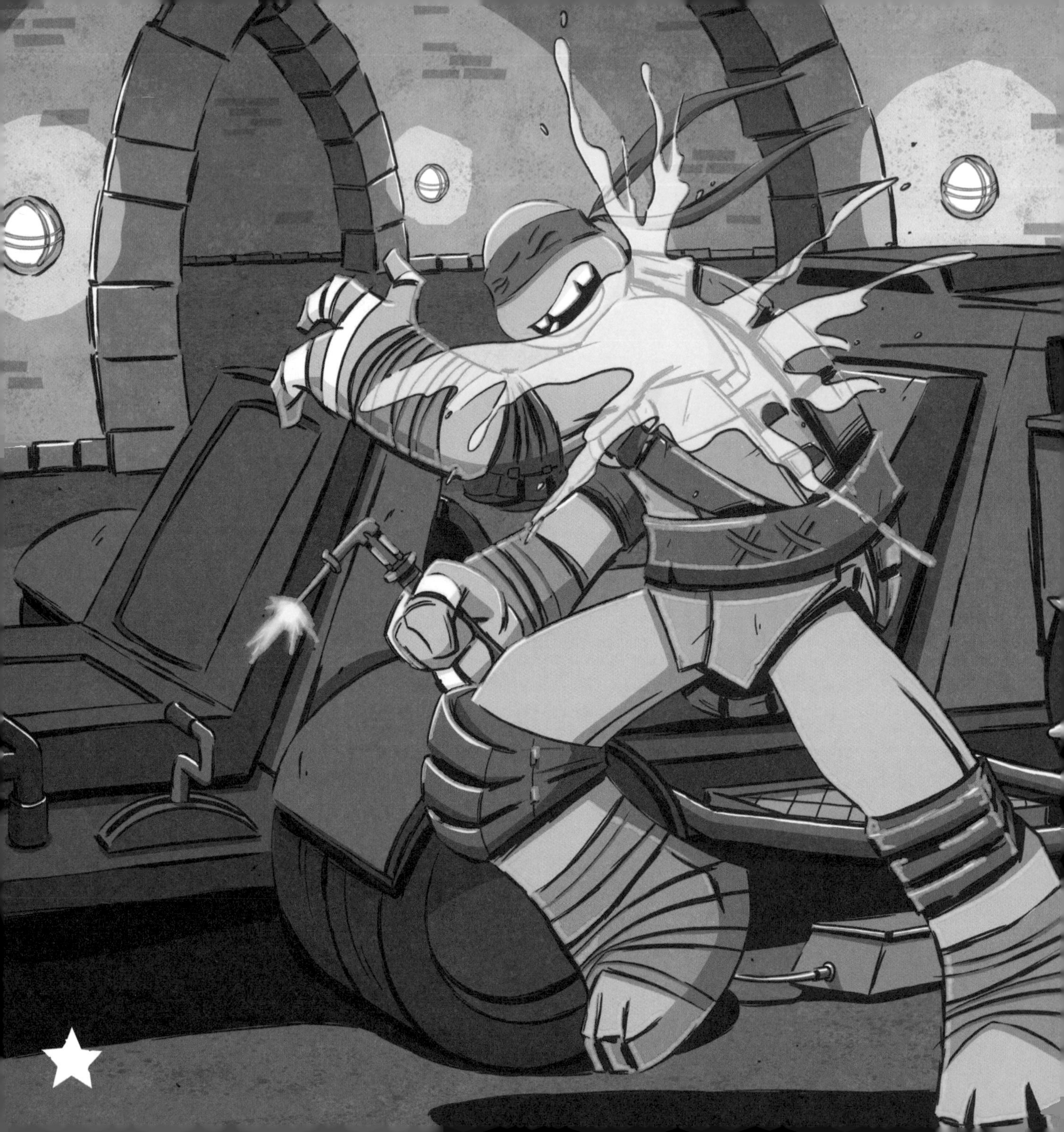

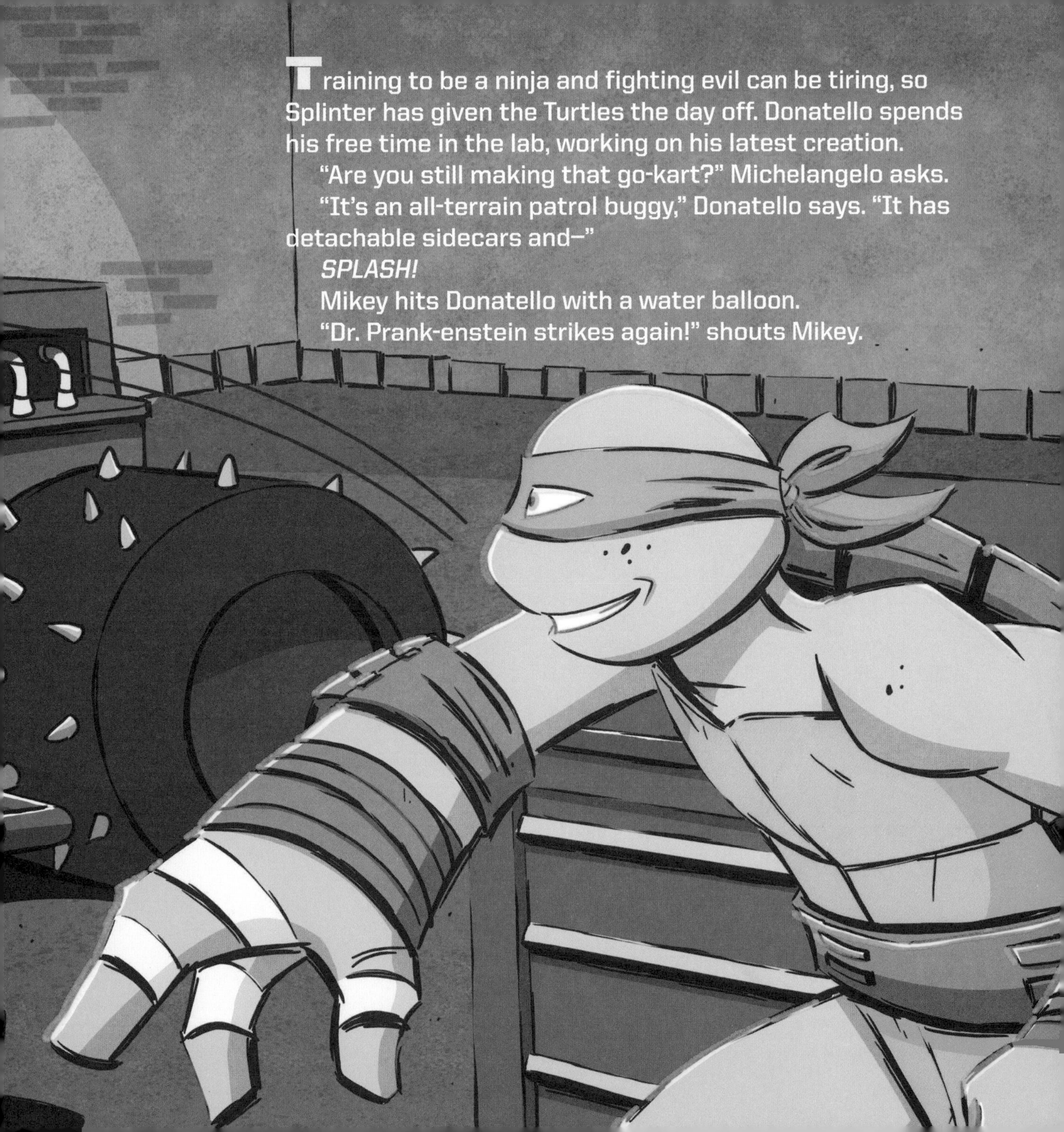

Training to be a ninja and fighting evil can be tiring, so Splinter has given the Turtles the day off. Donatello spends his free time in the lab, working on his latest creation.

"Are you still making that go-kart?" Michelangelo asks.

"It's an all-terrain patrol buggy," Donatello says. "It has detachable sidecars and—"

SPLASH!

Mikey hits Donatello with a water balloon.

"Dr. Prank-enstein strikes again!" shouts Mikey.

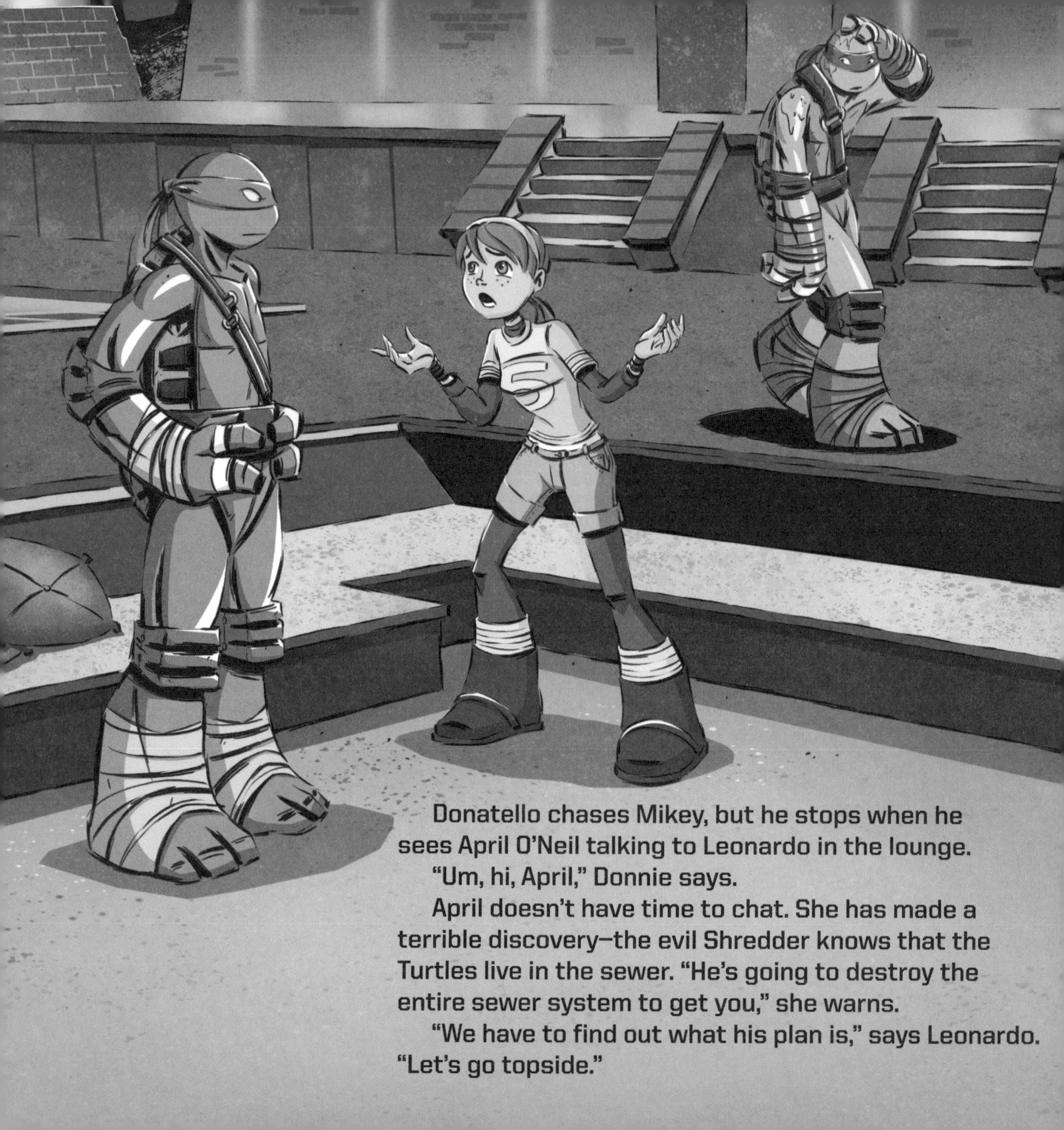

Donatello chases Mikey, but he stops when he sees April O'Neil talking to Leonardo in the lounge.

"Um, hi, April," Donnie says.

April doesn't have time to chat. She has made a terrible discovery—the evil Shredder knows that the Turtles live in the sewer. "He's going to destroy the entire sewer system to get you," she warns.

"We have to find out what his plan is," says Leonardo. "Let's go topside."

April leads the Turtles to the warehouse where Shredder is hatching his fiendish plot. To get inside, she pretends to deliver a pizza.

"I don't like giving free pizza to the bad guys," whispers Michelangelo.

The bad guys aren't fooled—they capture April!

"We've got to save her!" Donatello shouts.

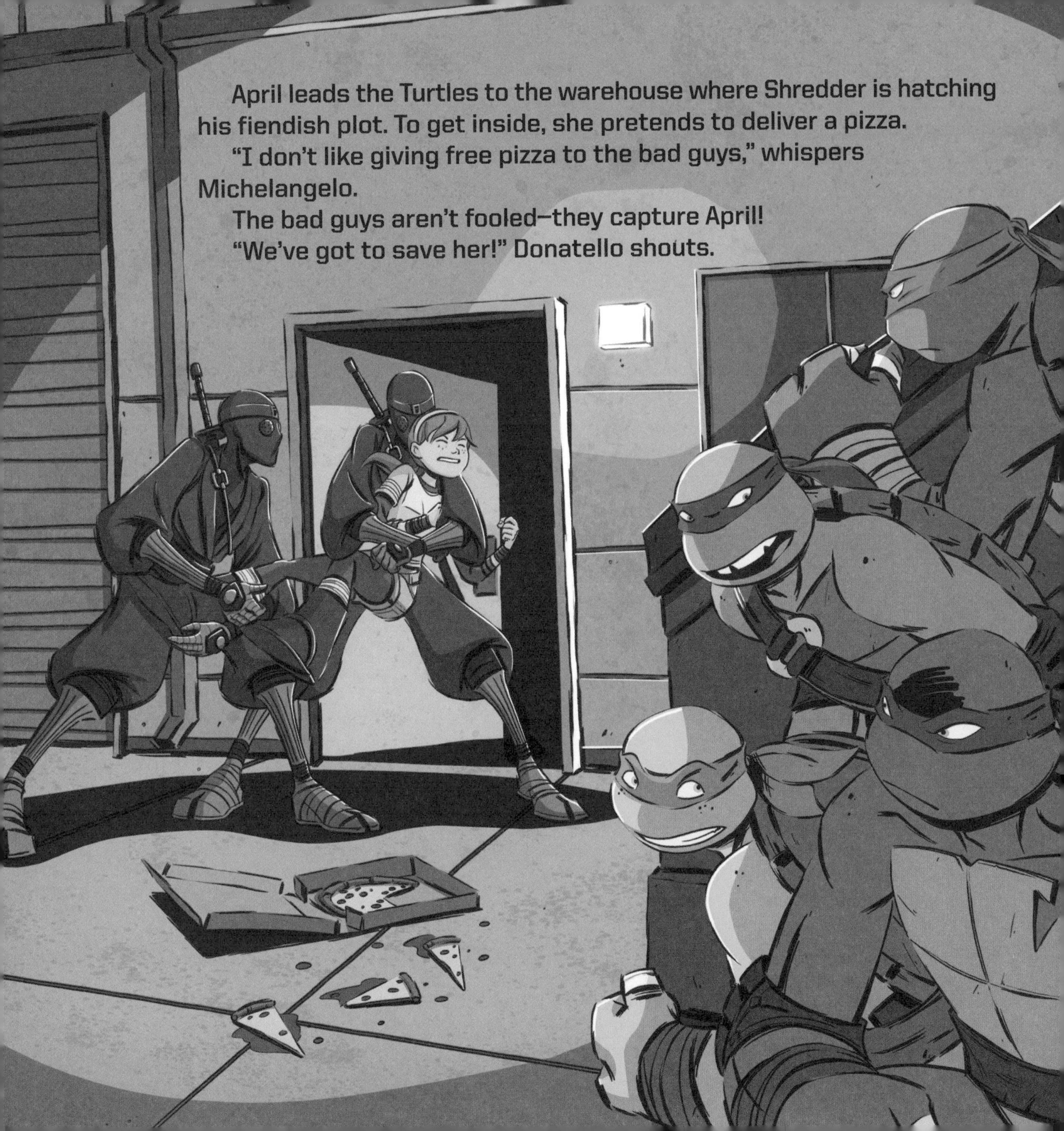

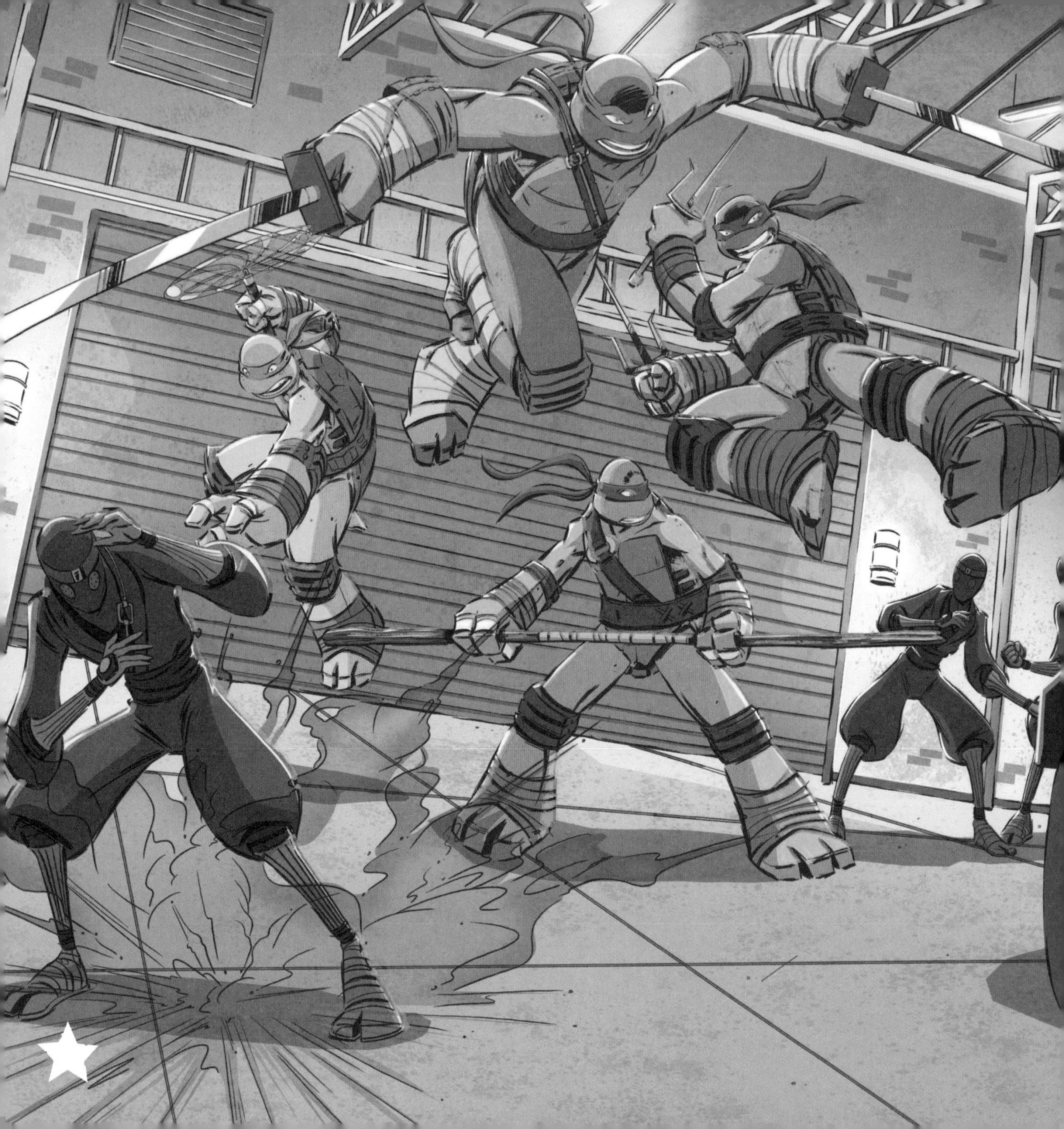

The Turtles creep into the warehouse and see Shredder's ninja henchmen, the Foot Clan, filling a giant tanker truck with a strange chemical.

The battle is on! Leonardo swings his shining double swords. Raphael charges with his *sais*!

The giant tanker truck roars to life, and Michelangelo hurls a smoke bomb to stop it.

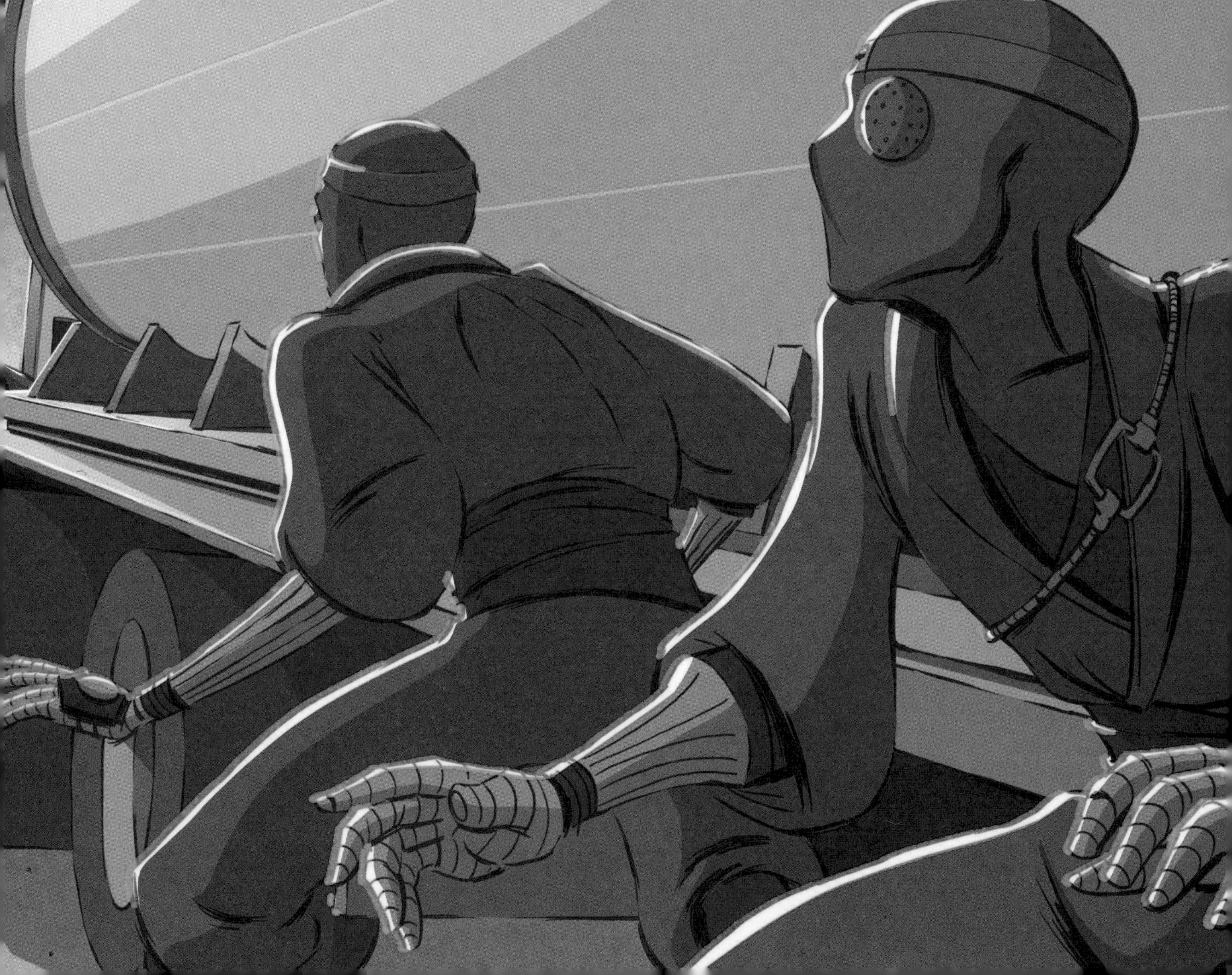

The Turtles can't stop the Foot Clan. April is driven away in a white van. The tanker thunders into the night.

"I figured out Shredder's plan," says Donnie. "That tanker is carrying a dangerous chemical. When mixed with water, it explodes. If it's poured into the sewer, everything will blow up—including our lair!"

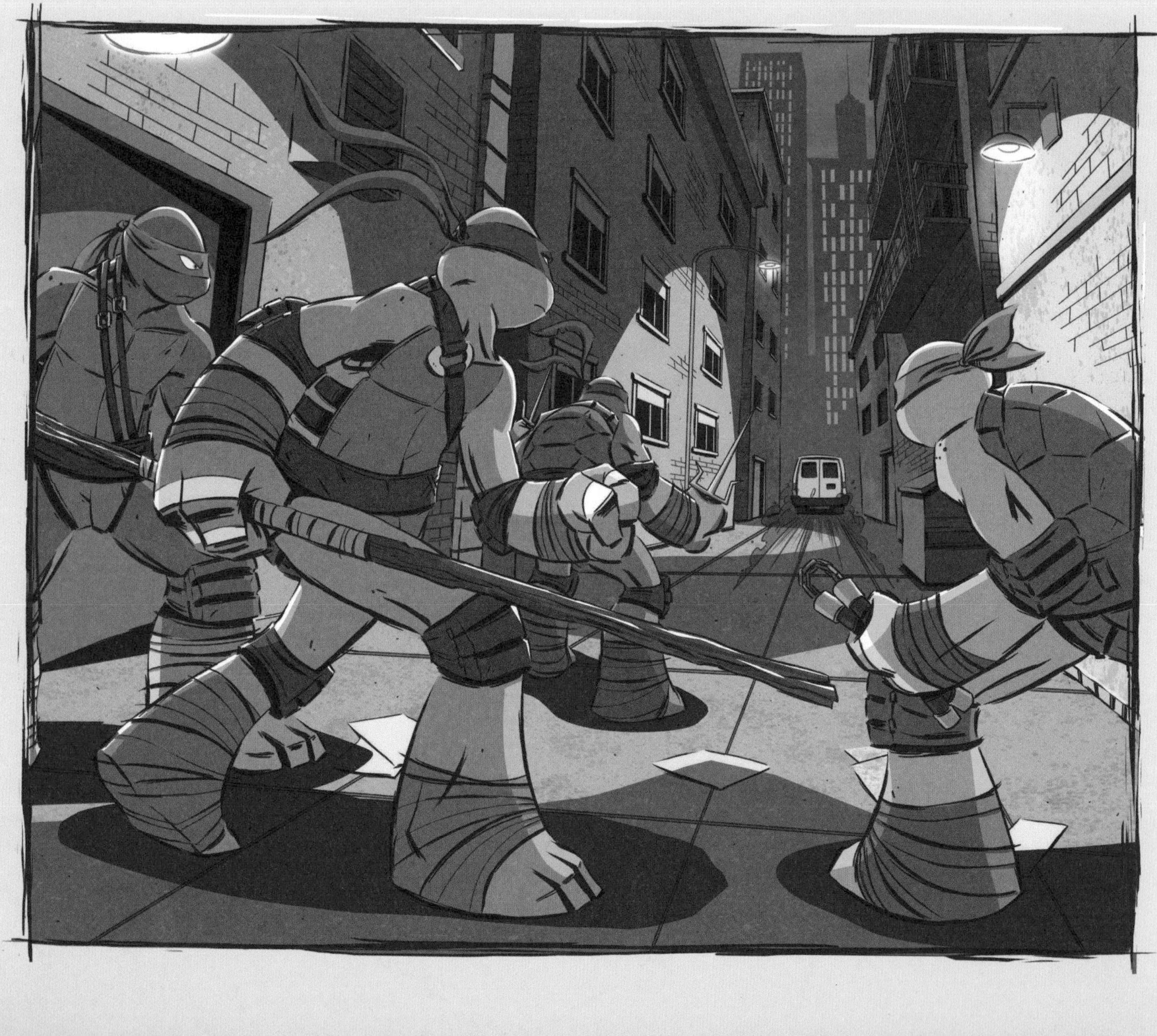

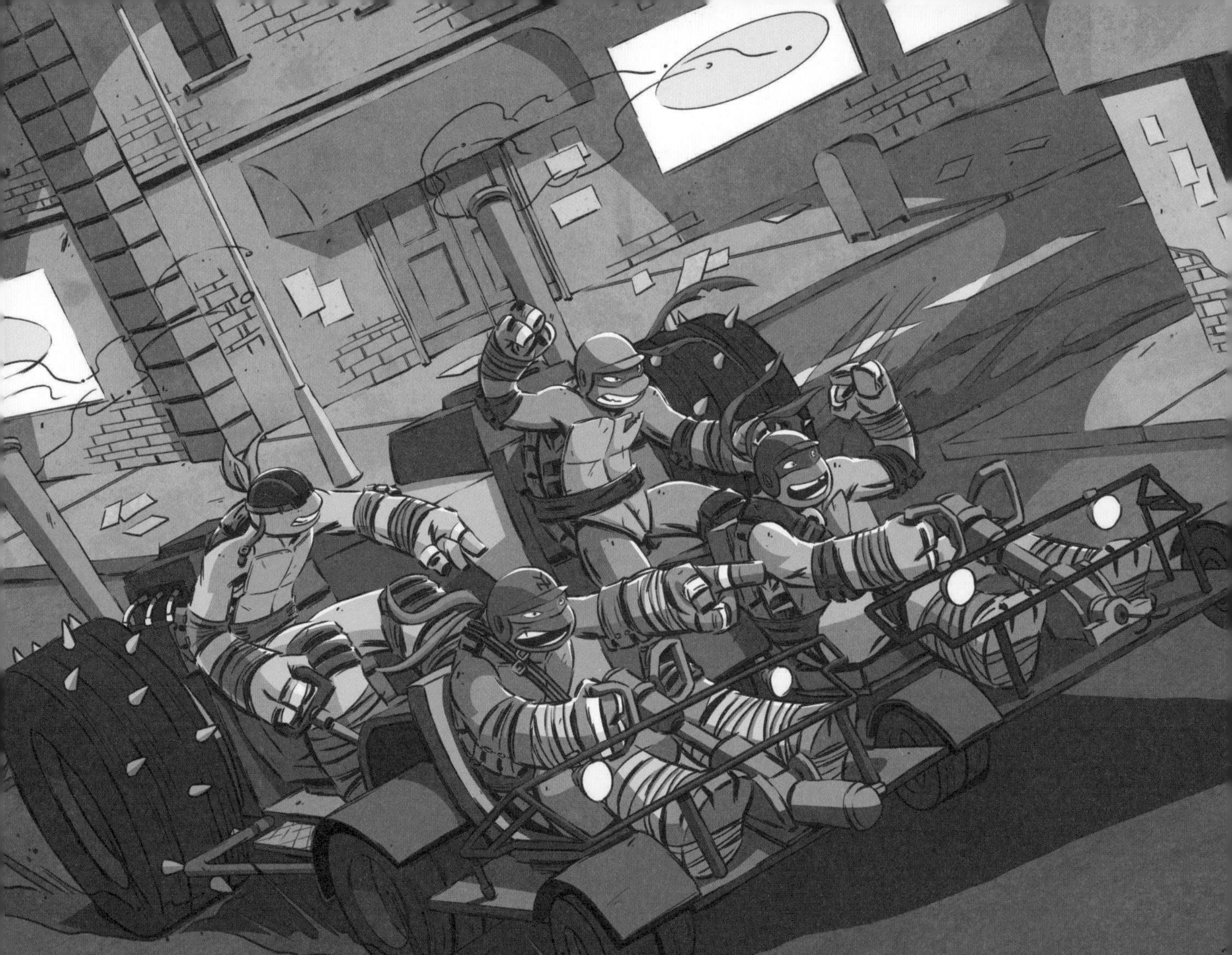

“We’ll never be able to save April and stop the tanker on foot,” says Donatello.

“We’re not going on foot,” says Leonardo.

The Turtles run back to the lair and get Donnie’s patrol buggy. It zooms through the city.

“Does this thing have a radio?” asks Michelangelo.

The Turtles' buggy skids around a corner. The tanker is coming directly toward them! Leo speeds up.

"Watch this," he says, pulling a lever.

The buggy splits in half. Leo and Mikey swerve to one side of the tanker. Raphael and Donnie race to the other side.

"We'll go find April," Raphael yells.

"And we'll stop the tanker," Leo shouts back.

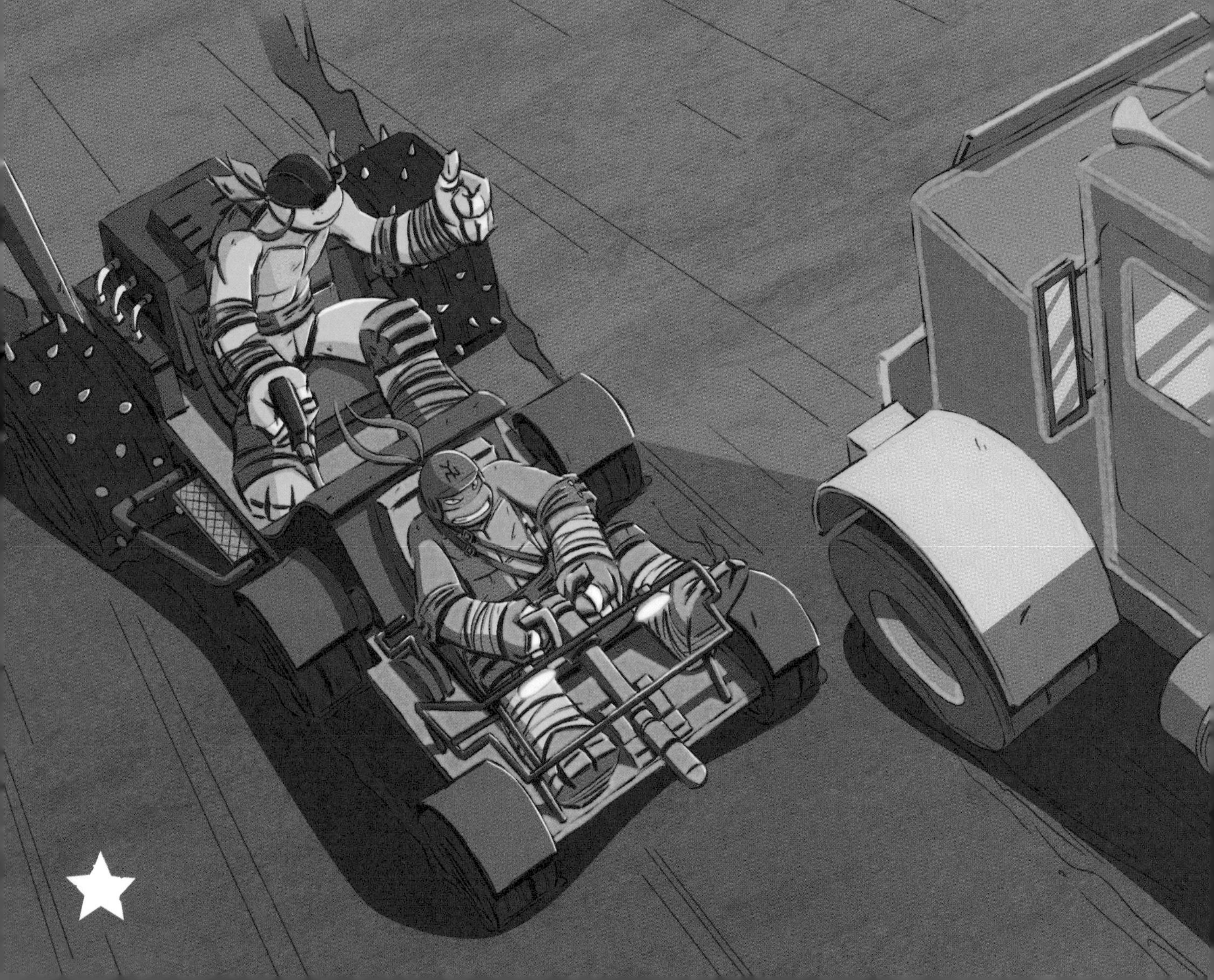

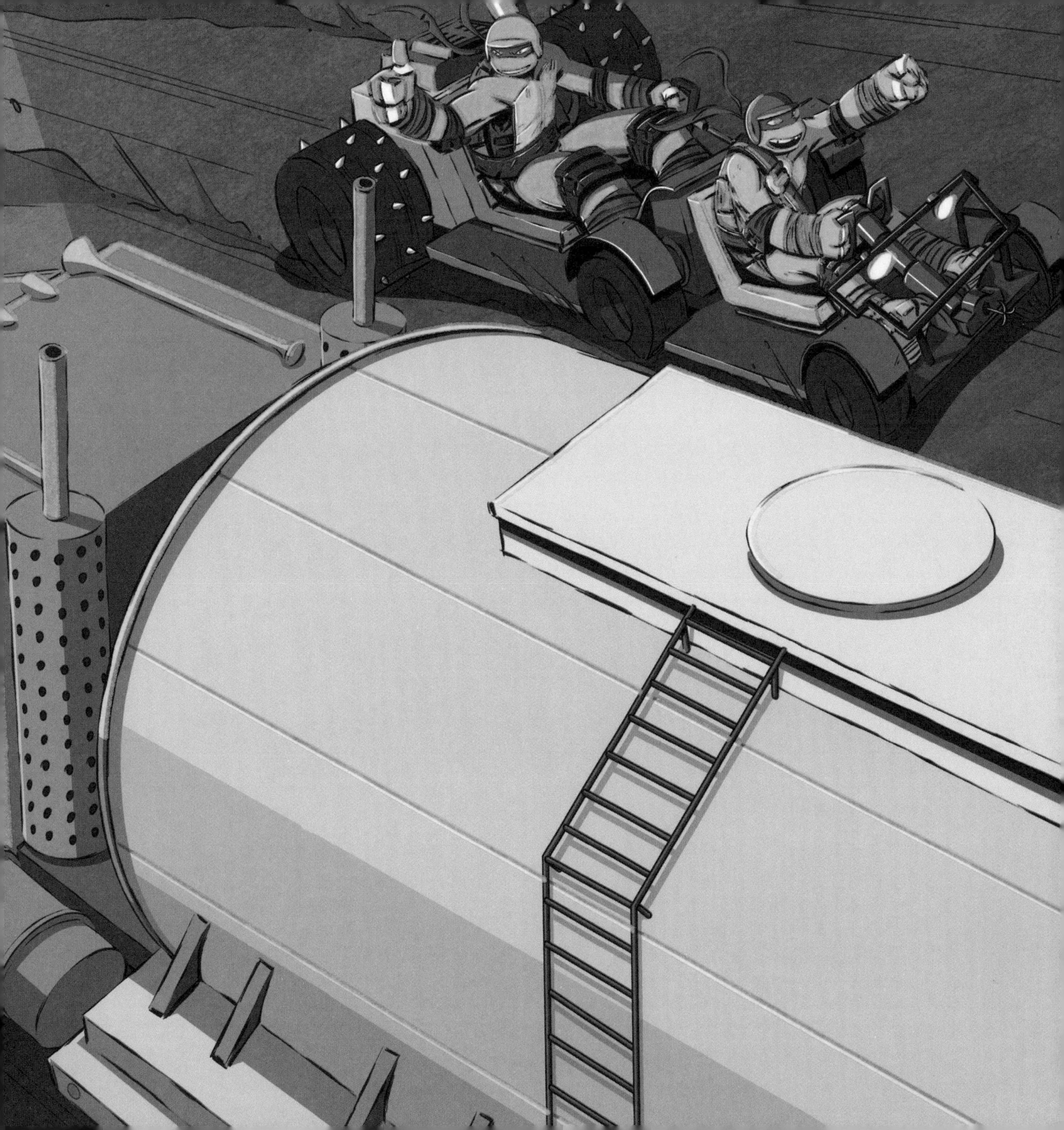

Donnie and Raphael find the van. Donnie hurls a throwing star and blows out a tire. The van skids to a stop. The two Turtles make quick work of the Foot Clan ninjas in a blaze of *ninjutsu*.

"Thanks," says April.

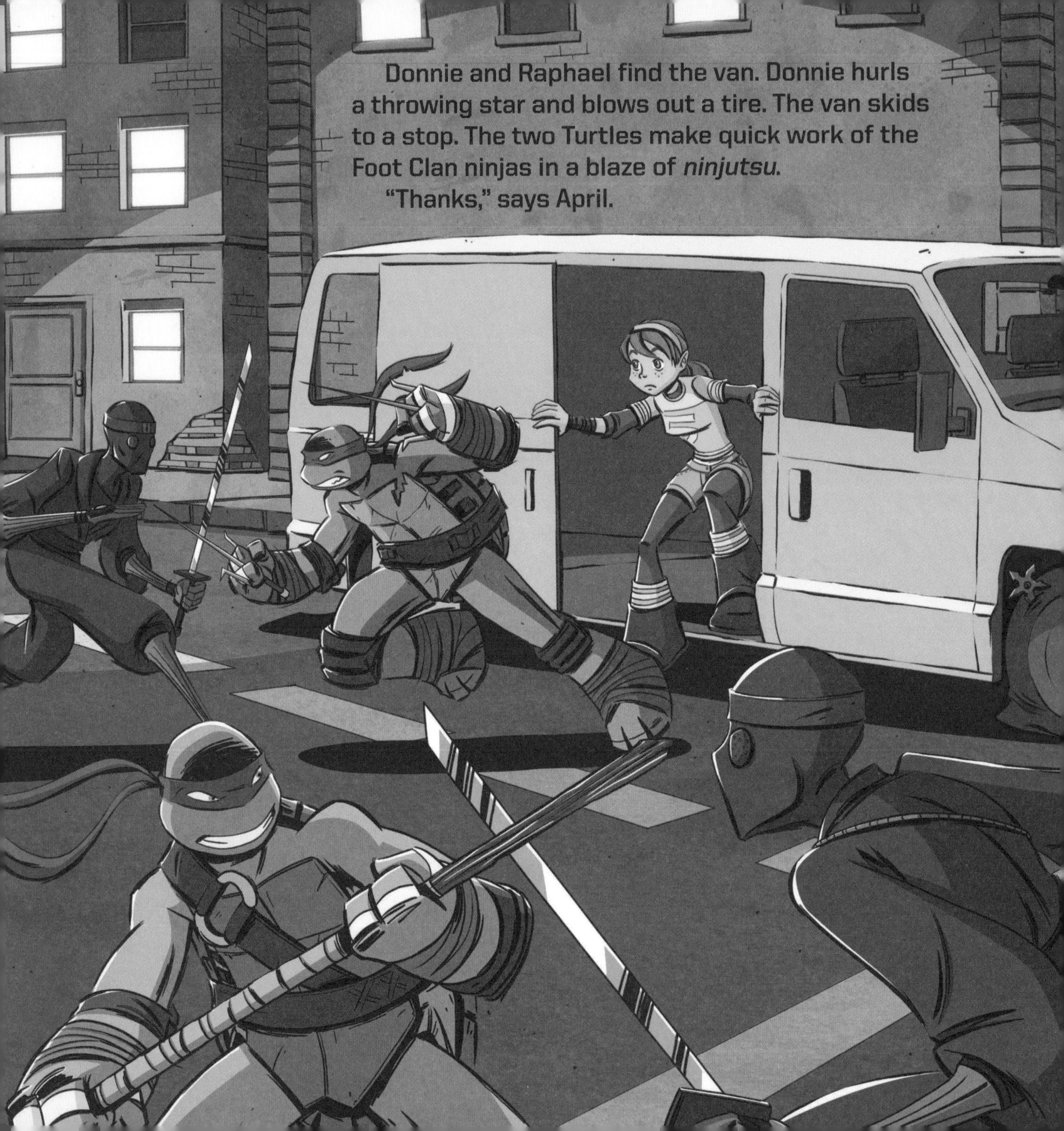

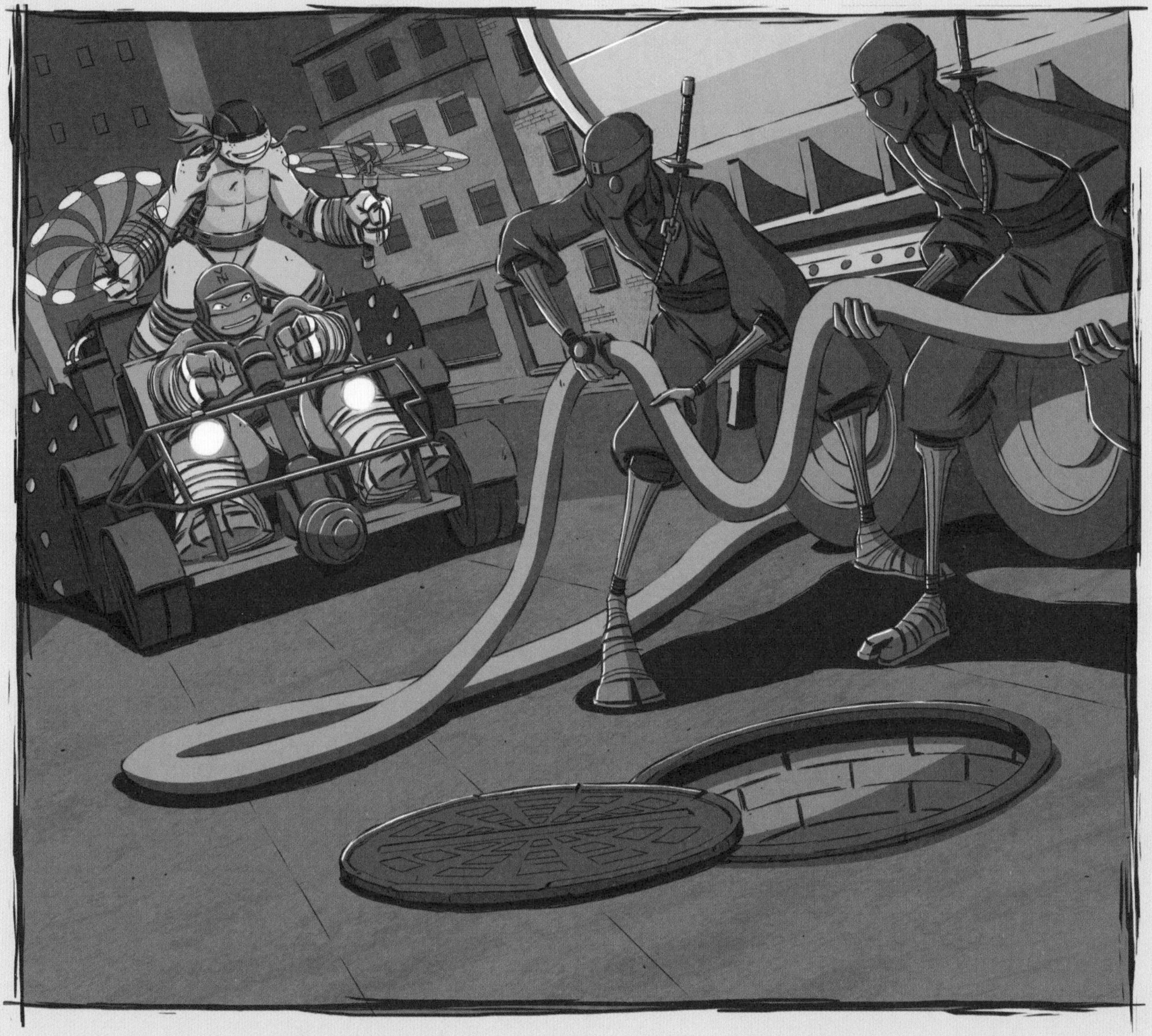

A few blocks away, Mikey and Leo find the tanker. The bad guys are carrying a hose from the tanker to an open manhole. They're going to pump the chemical into the sewer.

"We have to stop them!" Leonardo yells. "Do you have any water balloons, Mikey?"

Michelangelo smiles. "I sure do."

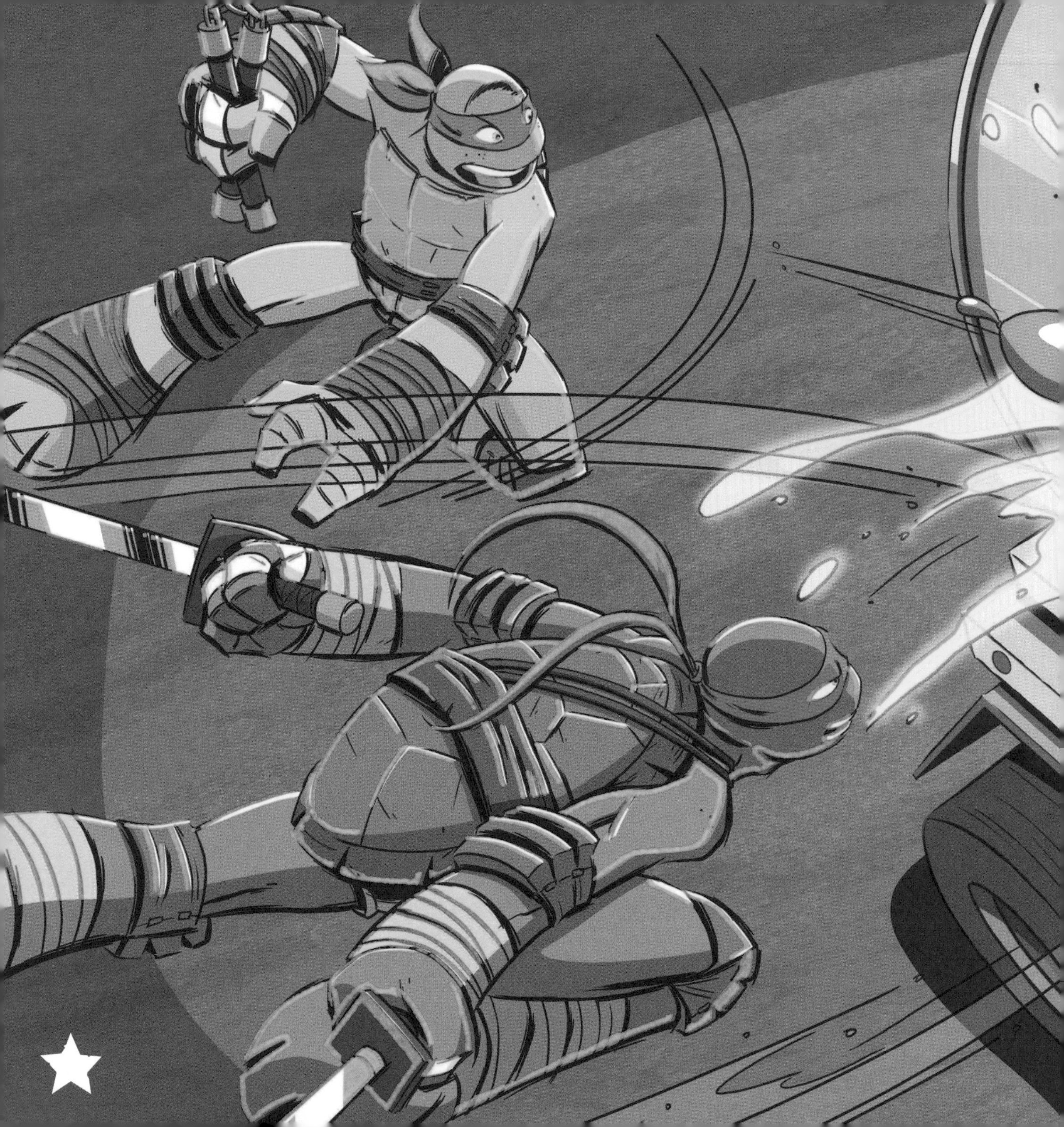

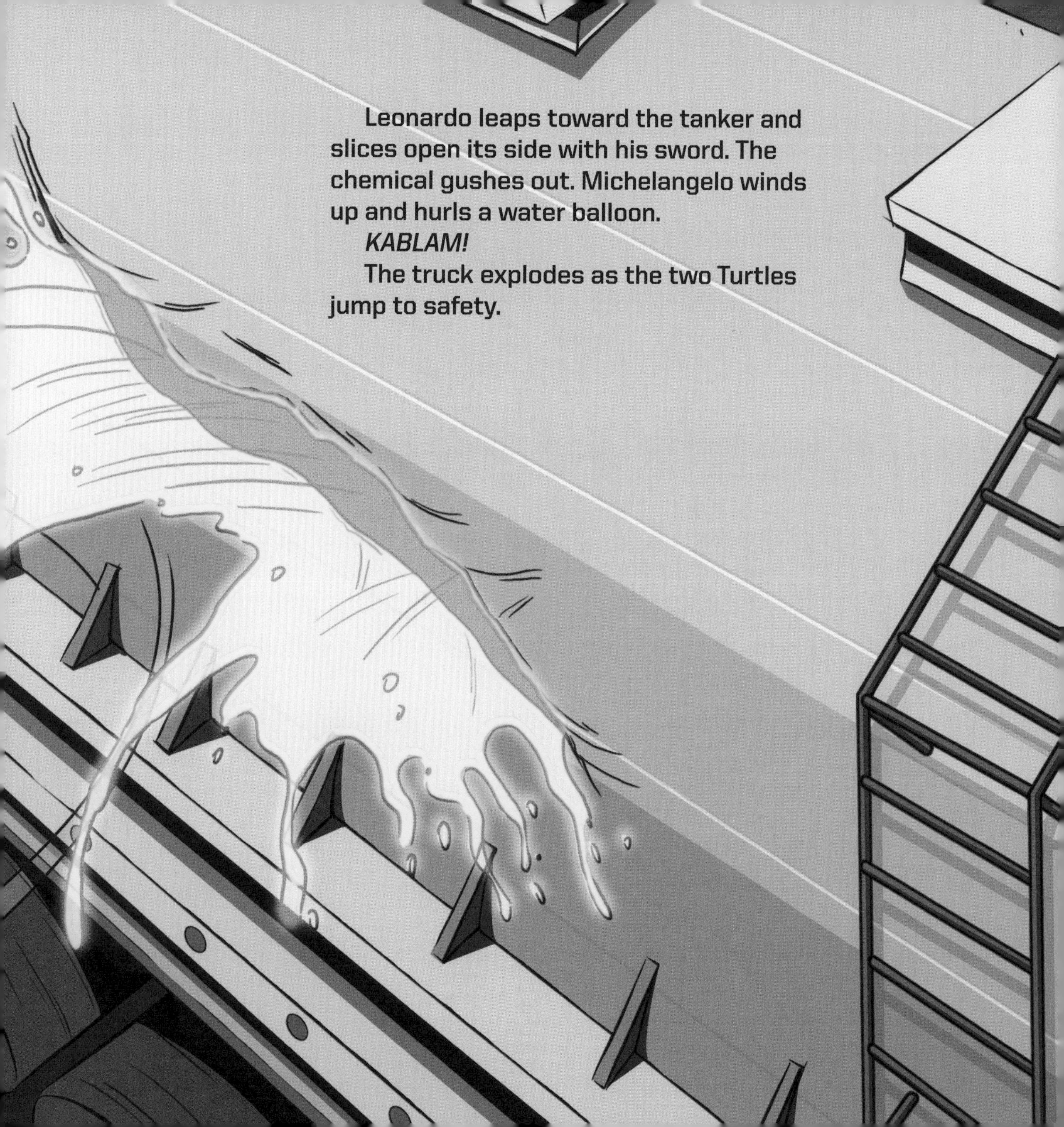

Leonardo leaps toward the tanker and slices open its side with his sword. The chemical gushes out. Michelangelo winds up and hurls a water balloon.

KABLAM!

The truck explodes as the two Turtles jump to safety.

The Turtles and April return to the lair to celebrate with pizza.
"This pizza smells kind of funky," says Donatello. "Where'd you get it, Mikey?"
"It's the one April dropped in the alley."
Everyone groans and throws their pizza back in the box—except Mikey.
"We live in a sewer," he says. "We can't be clean freaks! Oh well, more for me!"

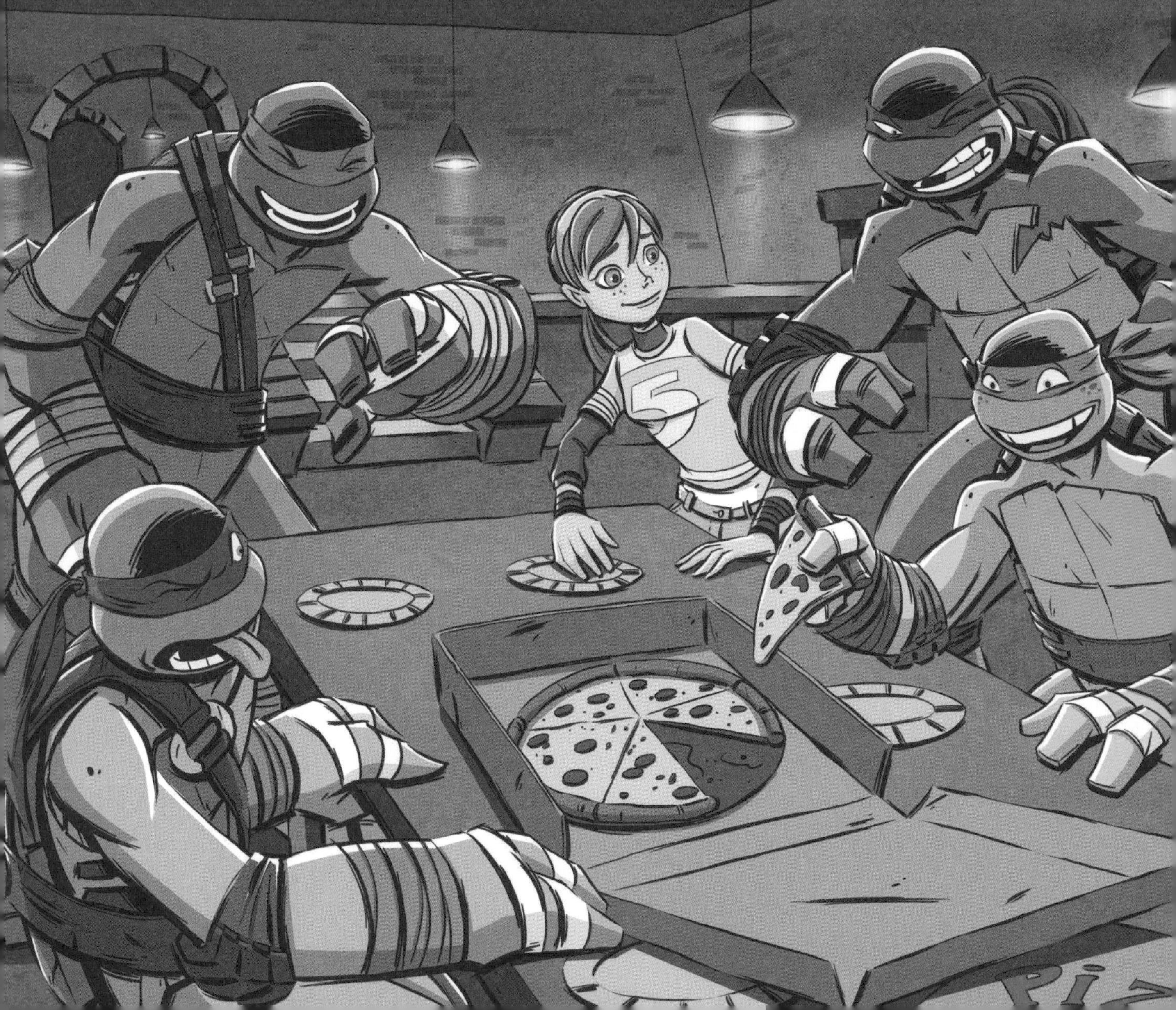